A Gold Star for George

Early★Reader

First American edition published in 2019 by Lerner Publishing Group, Inc.

An original concept by Alice Hemming
Copyright © 2020 Alice Hemming

Illustrated by Kimberley Scott

First published by Maverick Arts Publishing Limited

Maverick
arts publishing

Licensed Edition
A Gold Star for George

Lerner Publications Company
A division of Lerner Publishing Group, Inc.
241 First Avenue North
Minneapolis, MN 55401 USA

For reading levels and more information, look up this title at www.lernerbooks.com.

Main body text set in Mikado. Typeface provided by HVD Fonts.

Library of Congress Cataloging-in-Publication Data

Names: Hemming, Alice, author. | Scott, Kimberley, illustrator.
Title: A gold star for George / by Alice Hemming ; illustrated by Kimberley Scott.
Description: Minneapolis : Lerner Publications, [2019] | Series: Early bird readers. Orange (Early bird stories) | "The original picture book text for this story has been modified by the author to be an early reader." | Originally published in Horsham, West Sussex by Maverick Arts Publishing Ltd. in 2016.
Identifiers: LCCN 2018043773 (print) | LCCN 2018052759 (ebook) | ISBN 9781541561670 (eb pdf) | ISBN 9781541542075 (lb : alk. paper)
Subjects: LCSH: Readers (Primary) | Zoo animals—Juvenile literature. | Awards—Juvenile literature.
Classification: LCC PE1119 (ebook) | LCC PE1119 .H4775 2019 (print) | DDC 428.6/2—dc23

LC record available at https://lccn.loc.gov/2018043773

Manufactured in the United States of America
1-45392-39008-11/13/2018

A Gold Star for George

Alice Hemming

Illustrated by **Kimberley Scott**

Lerner Publications ◆ Minneapolis

There was a new poster at the wildlife park.

GOLD STAR AWARD

Prizes for:

- Most Popular Animal

- Most Organized Animal

- Animal with the Best Tricks

- Best Dressed Animal

George hoped he would win a star.

He had never won a prize before.
A shiny gold star would look
perfect on his fence.

All the visitors loved the penguins.

So the penguins won the star

for being the most popular animal.

They had a big party.

George was happy for them.

The next star was for the most
organized animal.

George was always neat and tidy.

So George helped the lemurs to tidy up.

George was happy to help.

When the lemurs won the star,
George was glad.

Next was the gold star for the best trick. All the animals could do clever tricks.

But not George.

He tried magic tricks, but he couldn't hold the cards.

Handstands were impossible,
and he couldn't hula-hoop at all.

There was one star left for the best dressed animal.

George always looked sharp.
He hoped he would win.

But all the other animals wore
bow ties, just like George!

"Well done, Toni," said George to
the winner.

George wished he had won a gold star.

He was a little bit sad that night.

When George woke up, he heard
muttering and banging.

He saw something twinkling on his
fence. Something shiny!

There were lots and lots of gold stars!

Now George was a winner!

Quiz

1. Who wins the prize for being the most popular animal?
   a) The lemurs
   b) The penguins
   c) George the giraffe

2. Why can't George do magic tricks with cards?
   a) He can't hold them.
   b) He doesn't have any cards.
   c) He is not a magician.

3. How many stars do George's friends make for him?
   a) Three
   b) Four
   c) Five

4. What do the animals wear to try winning the Best Dressed Animal Award?

a) A shirt

b) A bow tie

c) A hat

5. Who wins the best tricks?

a) A monkey

b) A snake

c) A mouse

Leveled for Guided Reading

COLOR		GRL
Purple	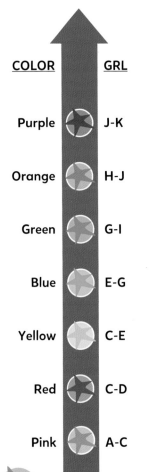	J-K
Orange		H-J
Green		G-I
Blue		E-G
Yellow		C-E
Red		C-D
Pink		A-C

Early Bird Stories have been edited and leveled by leading educational consultants to correspond with guided reading levels. The levels are assigned by taking into account the content, language style, layout, and phonics used in each book.